Project
Friendship

by Laurie Calkhoven
illustrated by Arcana Studios

★ American Girl®

Questions or comments? Call 1-800-845-0005,
visit **americangirl.com**, or write to Customer Service,
American Girl, 8400 Fairway Place, Middleton, WI 53562-0497.

Printed in China
13 14 15 16 17 18 LEO 10 9 8 7 6 5 4 3 2 1

Illustrated by Thu Thai at Arcana Studios

Welcome to Innerstar University! At this imaginary, one-of-a-kind school, you can live with your friends in a dorm called Brightstar House and find lots of fun ways to let your true talents shine. Your friends at Innerstar U will help you find your way through some challenging situations, too.

When you reach a page in this book that asks you to make a decision, choose carefully. The decisions you make will lead to more than 20 different endings! (*Hint:* Use a pencil to check off your choices. That way, you'll never read the same story twice.)

Want to try another ending? Read the book again—and then again. Find out what would have happened if you'd made *different* choices. Then head to www.innerstarU.com for even more book endings, games, and fun with friends.

Innerstar Guides

Every girl needs a few good friends to help her find her way. These are the friends who are always there for **you.**

Emmy

A brave girl who loves swimming and boating

Isabel

A confident girl with a funky sense of style

Riley

A good sport, on the field and off

Paige

A nature lover who leads hikes and campus cleanups

Amber

An animal lover and
a loyal friend

Neely

A creative girl who loves
dance, music, and art

Logan

A super-smart girl
who is curious about
EVERYTHING

Shelby

A kind girl who is there
for her friends—and loves
making NEW friends!

Innerstar U Campus

1. Rising Star Stables
2. Star Student Center
3. Brightstar House
4. Starlight Library
5. Sparkle Studios
6. Blue Sky Nature Center

[Y]ou're on your way to science class when you spot Logan and Paige hanging out near the sparkling fountain at Five-Points Plaza.

"Where are you off to?" Logan asks.

"Science," you say. "We're starting a new unit today in the lab. It should be fun!"

"We are, too, but not until later this afternoon," Paige says. "I can't wait to see what we're going to be studying."

You're not surprised that nature-loving Paige likes science. Logan probably does, too. She's curious about *everything,* and science is all about asking questions and finding answers. "I wish we were in the same lab," you say to your friends.

"We can still study together," Logan points out.

You give Logan a grateful smile. "Sounds good," you say. "I'd better get going, though. I don't want to be late!"

 Turn to page 10.

Science has become one of your favorite subjects, right up there with math. In your last lab, you did an experiment to see how your sense of smell affects your sense of taste. Once you even made fluorescent slime! You can't wait to see what experiment awaits you in lab today.

When you get to class, you take a seat near the front. There's a rack of safety goggles near your table, and you immediately try on a pair to see how they fit.

Devin, a redheaded girl with a mean streak, takes one look at you from the classroom doorway and starts to snicker. Her friend Alexis giggles, too, and you feel a blush creep up your cheeks as you quickly take off the goggles.

You're relieved to see Riley, a friend from soccer, coming into class just behind Devin. Then Nadia, a sweet, dark-haired girl, slips onto the stool next to yours with a shy smile. "Want to be lab partners?" she asks.

You know that Nadia struggles with math and maybe with science, too. You'd rather partner with Riley.

 If you say yes to Nadia, turn to page 12.

If you ask Riley instead, turn to page 13.

If you wait for the teacher's instructions, turn to page 14.

You don't know how to say
no to Nadia without hurting her
feelings. "Sure, I'd love to be your
lab partner," you say, cringing a
little inside.

"Thanks!" Nadia says.
"I know you're good at science.
Maybe you can even help *me* get a better grade."

Or maybe you'll bring my grade down, you think. But you
force a smile and decide to make the best of the situation.
You have enough confidence in your own science skills to
believe that you'll learn a lot in this unit, even if your
partner struggles a bit. Plus, you and Nadia can still study
with your friends Paige and Logan. Maybe Riley will join
you, too.

As your teacher, Ms. Blackwell, begins to talk about all
the cool things you're going to do and learn in this unit,
you get excited all over again. Even better, she's using real
scientific terms, like H_2O for water and *Homo sapiens* for
humans. You take careful notes while Ms. Blackwell talks
about proper scientific procedure and lab safety, but you
can tell that Nadia is a little overwhelmed.

"I hope you understood all that," she says, rubbing her
forehead. "I'm totally confused."

"Let's go over it after dinner tonight," you suggest.

 Turn to page 15.

"Um, thanks," you say to Nadia, "but I was just about to ask Riley to be my partner. She's a good friend of mine." Nadia looks a little disappointed, but she quickly moves across the room to ask someone else.

You're excited when Riley agrees to be your partner. You've always admired her. Not only is she a super athlete, but she's super smart, too.

Partnering with Riley turns out to be fun—and easy. She's a science whiz like you, so you alternate taking the lead on experiments. You trust Riley's science skills and are grateful to have such a strong partner.

Things get even better when your teacher announces that the Innerstar U Science Fair will be next month. "You can each enter on your own or with a partner," Ms. Blackwell says.

"What do you say?" asks Riley. "Wouldn't it be fun to do a project together?"

You're flattered that Riley wants to be partners for the science fair, and you figure that if you two put your heads together, you'll have a pretty good shot at winning. You have some ideas for projects that you've been wanting to try, but will Riley like your ideas?

 If you share an idea with Riley, turn to page 21.

If you ask her what she's thinking about doing, turn to page 19.

You don't want to insult Nadia by saying no, but you're not sure she's the right lab partner for you. "Are you sure we can choose our own partners?" you ask. "Maybe we should wait for the teacher's instructions."

Nadia shrugs, and a moment later, you see her walk across the room and ask someone else. By the time the teacher, Ms. Blackwell, arrives, it seems as if everyone has already partnered up.

"Does anyone still need a lab partner?" she asks.

Only one other girl raises her hand—Devin. *Uh-oh.* You try to keep the dismay from showing on your face, but the last person in this room that you want to partner up with is Devin.

"Hey, partner," she says, waving you toward her lab table in the back of the room.

If you go back and join her, turn to page 16.

If you wave her up to your table in the front row, turn to page 25.

Nadia has so many extracurricular activities—art class, dance class, and drama club—that it's pretty late when she knocks on your door for a study session.

By the time you go over the work you did in science lab and discuss the chapter you were assigned to read, you're yawning like crazy. When Nadia pulls out her math homework and asks for your help with that, too, you sigh. You'd much rather go to bed.

"I just wanted to ask you something quick," she says. "What did you get for problem number three?"

You open your own notebook and scan your work. "Seventeen," you say with another big yawn.

"Hmm," she says. "I got fifteen."

You take a quick look and see that Nadia got almost *all* the answers wrong. You try to explain the correct way to do the problems, but you can tell that she still doesn't get it. You're too tired to keep trying tonight, so you let Nadia jot down your answers—after she promises that she'll work through the problems again on her own in the morning.

 Turn to page 18.

You force yourself to smile as you join Devin in the back row. For the next hour, while Ms. Blackwell is talking about lab safety, Devin is doodling pictures of horses in her notebook or writing notes to her friends Alexis and Madison.

You're feeling pretty bummed about your new partnership, but after class, Devin invites you to go to dinner later with her and her friends. You say yes, mostly because Devin caught you by surprise and you don't know what else to say.

Over dinner, Devin and her friends talk about horseback riding, something you've never done. But the girls promise to help you get started. They've even decided which horse at Rising Star Stables would be right for you.

"Angel is super sweet," says Alexis. "You'll love her!"

"Wait, what do you know about choosing horses?" Devin snaps at Alexis. "Aren't you the one who fell off your horse during the last competition?"

There's the Devin you remember—the one who's nice, right up until the moment when she isn't.

Alexis's cheeks flush and she looks down at her plate. You're wondering if you should speak up on her behalf when Paige and Logan walk by with their trays.

"Geek alert," Devin mutters under her breath.

Your own cheeks flush now. Did Logan and Paige hear her?

🌟 Turn to page 37.

Nadia's not good at math, but she turns out to be a great science-lab partner. She's happy to let you take the lead on experiments—something you love to do—while she keeps the lab notes. She waits patiently for you to tell her exactly what to write. It crosses your mind that maybe you're letting Nadia lean on you a little *too* much. But you're learning a lot and having fun, and you tell yourself that Nadia is, too.

Math is a different story. Nadia comes to you nearly every night with her homework. You understand the work, but you don't seem to be very good at teaching it to your friend. Often you end up just giving her the answers.

"Do you want me to speak to the teacher for you?" you ask. "Maybe you can get some extra help."

"No!" Nadia says, her cheeks flaming. "Please don't tell her."

You don't understand why Nadia is so embarrassed, but you agree to keep her secret. You wonder, though, if maybe there's another way to help her.

 If you decide to ask the teacher to explain things more slowly, turn to page 22.

 If you keep giving Nadia the answers, turn to page 39.

"Do you have ideas for the science fair?" you ask.

"I have a couple," Riley says, thinking. "I've noticed that soccer balls fly higher or farther depending on how much air is in them. I thought we could test balls with different air pressures and see how they do."

You're not crazy about that idea, but you don't let it show. "Interesting," you say slowly. "What else?"

"Or we could test how exercise affects brainpower," Riley says.

You like that idea better—it seems more scientific. But you get the impression that Riley is more interested in her soccer-ball experiment. Still, though, you think your own ideas are more likely to win. Will Riley be insulted if you start offering your ideas?

 If you vote for exercise and brainpower, turn to page 42.

 If you suggest an idea of your own, turn to page 21.

If you support Riley's soccer-ball idea but do something of your own on the side, turn to page 36.

The flyer that Nadia hands you reads *Get Inspired!* It invites girls to create a piece of art—a painting, photograph, sculpture, or collage—based on something that inspires them.

"Sounds fun," you say, "but I'm just not very creative." You hand the flyer back to Nadia.

She pauses for a moment, her brown eyes thoughtful. Then she says, "You've been helping me with math and science—a *lot*. Maybe I can help you with art."

 If you tell Nadia that you'd rather stick with science, turn to page 57.

 If you agree to let Nadia help you with art, turn to page 59.

"What if we put some plants in a sunny window and others in one of our closets?" you suggest. "We can watch how they grow and prove that plants are healthiest when they get lots of sunlight."

Riley nods, but she doesn't leap on your idea. "That sounds okay," she says, "but I'm really more interested in testing something to do with sports or exercise."

Sports or exercise? Those subjects just don't sound very scientific to you. Riley must be able to read the look on your face because she says, "Maybe we should each do our own experiments so that we can study what we're really interested in. What do you think?"

 If you decide to do your own project, turn to page 23.

 If you decide to partner with Riley in the exercise experiment, turn to page 42.

You understand the work you're doing in math, but Nadia doesn't. So the next day in class, you raise your hand over and over again, asking the teacher, Ms. Williams, to slow down and explain things.

That's a little embarrassing for you—you've always gotten good grades in math, and you don't like being seen as someone who doesn't understand. But this is the only way you can think of to get Nadia extra help and keep her secret at the same time.

After class, Ms. Williams asks you to stay behind for a minute.

"Is there something wrong?" she asks nicely. "I know from your homework that you understand these concepts. You're one of my best students, but suddenly you seem confused."

You're really tempted to tell Ms. Williams what you've been trying to do, but you don't want to break your promise to Nadia.

"I just got a little turned around," you tell her. "But I understand now."

🌟 Turn to page 26.

You nod—you agree with Riley that you should each do a project of your own. You're sorry not to be working with your friend, but you're much more interested in studying plants than exercise or sports.

"We can still cheer each other on," Riley says, always the good sport, and that makes you feel better.

You gather your materials—ten small bean plants—from the Blue Sky Nature Center and set them up in your room. Five go on your sunny windowsill, and the other five go into your dark closet. Over the next two weeks you give them all the same amount of water and measure their growth. You also take lots of pictures.

The plants in the closet are definitely less healthy. They're not as green as the ones on the windowsill, and they're also longer and thinner, as if they're reaching out for light and can't find it. You decide to use that as the title for your presentation: "Reaching for the Light."

 Turn to page 29.

You wave Devin to the front row. With Ms. Blackwell watching, Devin doesn't have a choice about joining you, but you can tell by her frown that she isn't exactly thrilled to be sitting this close to the teacher.

Five minutes into the lesson about lab safety, you realize why. Devin spends most of her time drawing pictures of horses. She's not a bad artist, but that's not going to help you learn science—not unless you study the life cycle of a horse!

You're relieved when Ms. Blackwell notices and asks Devin to pay attention. Devin turns a page in her notebook and starts taking real notes. But when you raise your hand to ask the teacher a question, you see Devin look over her shoulder and make a face—no doubt making fun of you.

After Ms. Blackwell gives you your first homework assignment, Devin leans over to ask you something. "Hey," she says, "I'm busy tonight and won't have much time for homework. Do you think we could compare our answers before class tomorrow?"

 Turn to page 30.

You're so embarrassed when you leave math class that you decide you have to be yourself in class from now on. You can't pretend you don't understand the concepts anymore. You want to live up to Ms. Williams's belief in you.

But then you find Nadia waiting for you outside. She's both relieved and grateful that you asked so many questions, and she's not the only one. Your friend Neely stops you on your way back to Brightstar House.

"You were so helpful in math class today," she said. "I was a little confused, too, but I couldn't even figure out what questions to ask. Listening to you and Ms. Williams, suddenly everything clicked!"

You wonder if the work you've done with Nadia is finally paying off—teaching you how to be a teacher. At least *one* girl benefited from your questions and Ms. Williams's patient answers.

 If you decide to keep asking questions in math class, turn to page 28.

 If you decide to set up a study group to help your classmates, turn to page 32.

You continue to raise your hand in math class and ask basic questions, but you still feel embarrassed about it. You went from being a star math student to one who hides her talents. You even get a couple of homework questions wrong on purpose so that Ms. Williams doesn't suspect anything.

Meanwhile, Nadia continues to struggle. The more you try to help her, the less confident she seems. She's still copying your homework answers every night, and you know that will backfire on her when you have your next test.

You're in a real bind. Keeping Nadia's secret is getting tougher for you, and you're beginning to wonder if hiding her problem is hurting her more than helping her.

When you meet for your usual study session and she asks to see your homework, you hesitate.

If you let her see your answers, as usual, turn to page 39.

If you refuse to give her the answers, turn to page 38.

You and Riley get together to work on your posters about a week before the science fair. You have lots of charts and photos, and you think your project might be a winner.

"Remember to make your headline really big," Riley says. "We'll want girls in the audience to be able to see it."

Audience? You get a nervous feeling in the pit of your stomach. You never stopped to think about having to talk about your experiment in front of the judges—in front of a whole crowd. What if your presentation is a total flop?

You try to put your worries out of your mind, but they keep popping back in. That night, you dream about the science fair. You're standing in front of a huge crowd, and you can't talk. You're opening your mouth, but nothing's coming out.

The next night you have the same nightmare, and again the next. When you think about the science fair during the day, your hands get clammy and your mouth dries up. You even can feel your heart beating way too fast.

 If you drop out of the science fair because you're too stressed out, turn to page 31.

 If you practice your presentation with Riley and your other friends, turn to page 34.

If you ask your friends for advice, go online to innerstarU.com/secret and enter this code: TRY2BCONFIDENT

Devin said the word *compare*, but you're pretty sure she meant *copy*. You definitely don't want Devin copying your homework. You take a deep breath and look her right in the eye. "I'm not going to do your homework for you," you say quietly. "But if you want to work together tonight, we can do that."

Devin gives you a sharp look. "Fine," she says curtly. "I'll stop by after dinner."

You're not surprised but you're a little sad when Devin *doesn't* show up that night as she said she would. It's going to be a long semester if your science partner expects you to do all the work instead of her working *with* you.

 Turn to page 40.

You don't see how you can take part in the science fair if you can't shake this anxiety. You're convinced that your presentation will be a disaster and you'll look like a loser in front of the whole school!

Riley tries to talk you out of quitting, but it's no use. Two days before the science fair, you pull your project from the lineup. But you tell Riley that you'll still cheer her on at the fair, just as you promised.

The science fair takes place at the Market, which has been cleared of all its tents and is now full of girls, judges, tables, and posters. As you walk around looking at the posters, you admire all the great ideas, but you can't help feeling a little sad. You had a great idea, too—a potential winner.

You stand by Riley's table while she presents her soccer-ball experiment to the judges. You're surprised when super-confident Riley gets flustered and messes up the beginning of her speech. But when she takes a deep breath, smiles, and starts over, you're impressed. She kept going and fought through her fear, whereas *you* let your insecurities get the best of you.

In that moment, you make the decision to build your confidence by speaking up more in class and by taking a stand for your good ideas. Next year, you're going to make sure *your* science-fair project gets counted.

The End

Neely's comments about how you helped her with math give you an idea. Maybe you can help Nadia and your other friends at the same time.

"How about doing a study group?" you ask. "Maybe we can all meet tonight and figure out our homework together."

"That's a great idea!" Neely says.

You think you see a look of dismay flit across Nadia's face, but then she smiles and agrees to join the study group. As the two of you walk back to your rooms in silence, you consider the questions you might ask about tonight's homework that will help the other girls—questions that you, of course, already know the answers to.

That night, in the study space in the attic of Brightstar House, you get the ball rolling with a few questions. When Neely gets stuck on something, you talk her through it.

"You're really good at this," Neely says. "Thanks so much for helping us."

Her words make you feel great, but you can see that Nadia is still struggling. She doesn't say a word during the study session, and after everyone has left the room, she asks once again for your homework.

🌟 Turn to page 38.

Your friends take turns practicing their presentations. You cheer them on, but when it's your turn to speak, your nightmare comes rushing back. Your mouth feels so dry that you're not sure you can form words. And forget about your hands—not only are your palms all sweaty, but when you try to point to your poster, you can see your hand shaking. Even your knees feel a little wobbly.

You think your project is a great one, but if you can't speak about it in front of your friends, how are you going to give a presentation to science-fair judges?

You're tempted to make a run for it, but first you take a deep breath, and then another. You look into the faces of your friends, and you can tell that every single one of them is interested in what you have to say and wants you to do well.

That gives you the courage to try again. After another deep breath, you begin. Your voice is a little shaky, but it gets stronger with every word. By the end of your practice presentation, you feel strong and confident.

"You did it!" says Riley, giving you a high five. "Do you feel better now?"

"I do!" you say, your voice loud and clear. You're ready to tackle the science fair—thanks to a little help from your friends.

The End

By the time Nadia arrives, you're nearly done with the experiment.

"Hey, you started without me," she says, sounding a little hurt.

"Yeah, and we'll be the first team to finish!" you say, trying to perk her back up.

Nadia reads over your notes while you measure the final ingredient—water.

"Now for the H_2O," you say to Nadia.

"Wait, I think you might have missed something," she says.

You're pretty sure you didn't—you know what you're doing. And you're eager to finish the experiment before anyone else does. That'll impress Ms. Blackwell. What do you do?

 If you put down the water and listen to what Nadia has to say, turn to page 95.

 If you go ahead and add the water, turn to page 96.

You agree to help Riley with her soccer-ball experiment, but during the rest of class, your mind wanders. You watch the class hamsters, Cheeks and Nibbles, running on their wheel, and that reminds you of a magazine article you just read about how hamsters' sense of smell is more powerful than their sense of sight. You'd love to do an experiment to explore that for yourself.

After class, you wait till Riley packs up her things and leaves, and then you approach Ms. Blackwell's desk to tell your teacher about the experiment you're hoping to do.

"I'd like to have Cheeks and Nibbles run in a maze," you say, "and I can help them along with different clues—some they can see and some they can smell."

"Sounds interesting," Ms. Blackwell says, "and I have just the thing to help you." She unlocks a supply cabinet near her desk and takes out an old wooden maze. It looks as if it's been used for lots of experiments, which you think is kind of exciting.

"You're welcome to keep the hamsters in your dorm room this coming weekend," says Ms. Blackwell, "after we spend some time talking about how to take good care of them," she adds with a wink.

 Turn to page 54.

"Hi!" Logan says, taking in the whole table. If she's surprised to see you sitting with Devin, she doesn't let it show. "We're going to meet in the attic in an hour to do our science homework. Want to join us?"

Devin cocks an eyebrow and waits for you to answer. You want to join Logan and Paige, but you feel as if this is a test. If you say yes, will Devin call you a geek and turn on you? Will she make your life in science lab miserable?

A minute ago you felt fine, but now you're feeling a little sick to your stomach.

If you say yes to Logan, turn to page 47.

If you say no to Logan, turn to page 44.

You take a deep breath. You know this can't go on any longer. "I'm sorry," you tell Nadia. "I can't give you the answers this time. You're not learning anything this way! What are you going to do when we have a test?"

Nadia looks surprised—she must not have expected this from you. Then her eyes flood with tears. "I'll fail the test, probably," she whispers.

You feel bad, but you don't understand why Nadia is being so stubborn about asking for real help. "Why don't you want Ms. Williams to know that you're struggling?" you ask outright.

Nadia shrugs, her lip quivering. "I guess I'm afraid that if I ask for help, she'll think I'm not smart or something," she says, her voice thick with tears.

"Or maybe she'll think you're *brave*," you counter. "Brave and confident enough to admit that you need help."

Nadia looks up at you, searching your eyes as if asking, *Are you sure?* "I never thought of it that way," she says, her voice sounding a little stronger.

You're relieved that Nadia seems to be listening to you. You're even more relieved when you walk into math class the next day and see Nadia talking with Ms. Williams. Nadia is smiling, which is a good sign.

When you catch her eye, you give her a thumbs-up: a vote of confidence for the girl who was finally brave enough to ask for help.

The End

You're afraid that if you stop sharing your homework with Nadia, she'll completely fail math class. So you hand over your answers for her to copy. She's getting by in class only because she's handing in *your* homework.

Still, you think you have everything under control—until Ms. Williams surprises your class with a pop quiz. You can tell by Nadia's tear-streaked face at the end of class that she didn't do well, and you know that it's partly your fault for covering for her.

Nadia runs out of class so quickly that you don't get a chance to talk to her. You're a little relieved—you're not even sure what you would say to her. Still, when Nadia doesn't show up for dinner at the student center, you wonder if you should try to find her.

 If you go to Nadia's room to talk things over, turn to page 48.

 If you wait for Nadia to come to you, turn to page 41.

The next day, you get to class early and take a seat in the front row again. Ms. Blackwell is there already, setting up the day's experiment.

"I'm glad you're early," she says. "How would you feel about changing lab partners? Devin and Alexis came to see me first thing this morning, and they'd really like to pair up. Would you mind working with Nadia?"

"*Really?* That would be great!" you say with a bit too much enthusiasm.

Ms. Blackwell gives you a questioning look, but you just smile. You're proud of yourself. You let Devin know that she couldn't bully you, and she heard you loud and clear and asked for a different lab partner. That means you can work with Nadia, whom you should have said yes to on the first day of lab.

You feel a twinge of worry, though, for Devin's new partner, Alexis. Devin will probably find a way to make her do all the work.

As the other students file into lab, you make a decision: You'll invite Alexis to study with you and Nadia. Who knows? Maybe while you're studying science, you can all learn a little bit about confidence and standing up to bullies, too.

The End

You think Nadia might be embarrassed and upset, so you don't seek her out. In fact, you don't see her again until math class the next morning. You try to get her attention, but she keeps her eyes on her desk throughout the lesson. You're beginning to think she's really mad at you.

Ms. Williams asks both you and Nadia to stay after class. When she hands back your quizzes, you quickly see that your answers are all correct—and Nadia's are nearly all wrong.

"I know you've been studying together," Ms. Williams says. "Can you explain this?"

Tearfully, Nadia explains that she was copying your homework answers.

Ms. Williams turns to you. "Have you been pretending not to understand the work in class so that Nadia would get some extra help?" she asks. Ms. Williams crosses her arms, waiting for your response.

 Turn to page 45.

You decide to team up with Riley on her exercise experiment. You think some of your own ideas might be stronger, but you don't want to outshine your lab partner. And anyway, it doesn't really matter whose idea you use. Teaming up with Riley will be fun!

When you hear that some of your friends are looking for science-project ideas, you share yours—the ones you won't be using. Then you and Riley design your experiment and recruit some of your friends to be test subjects.

You give each girl a list of math problems and ask her to do them right after lunch, when you've all been sitting for an hour or more. Later in the day—after classes and before dinner—you all go for a twenty-minute walk. Then your friends work through another set of math problems.

You expect the girls to work faster and smarter after some exercise, and that's mostly true. But one or two of your test subjects actually did better right after *lunch*.

 Turn to page 46.

Science class will be a nightmare if you and Devin aren't getting along. You muster up your courage and—without meeting Logan's eyes—say, "Actually, I think I'm going to study with these guys."

Devin gives you a smug smile, but Logan and Paige both seem confused by your response. Logan turns away a little too quickly, and Paige gives you an awkward wave before following Logan out of the cafeteria.

You watch your friends disappear around a corner, wondering if you did the right thing. Then Devin interrupts your thoughts by pushing her tray away and announcing, "Madison and I have some work to do at the stables. How about if you and Alexis get started on the science homework, and we can catch up with you later?"

Something about Devin's question doesn't feel quite right. You wonder if "get started" means "do all the work." But everyone is staring at you, and you hear yourself say, "Sure, sounds good."

 Turn to page 50.

"I made her promise not to tell," Nadia says, jumping to your defense.

You shake your head. "I messed up, too," you admit to Ms. Williams. "I let Nadia copy my answers, and I did pretend to struggle in class so that you would slow down a little." You swallow hard and glance at your feet.

Ms. Williams looks sternly from Nadia to you. "I don't know which is worse: keeping your struggles a secret"— she says to Nadia—"or pretending to be less than your best"—she says to you.

Ms. Williams has a solution for Nadia. "I'm going to sign you up to work with a real tutor," she says.

When Ms. Williams turns back to you, you hold your breath, waiting to hear your punishment.

"Letting a friend copy your work is never the right thing to do," your teacher begins. "That's cheating. But you did ask good questions that helped some of the other girls. So I'd like you to take a tutoring class and then lead a study group."

A study group? You're nervous and excited all at the same time. You weren't the right tutor for Nadia, but with some training, maybe you'll be able to help some of your other friends. Either way, you're done hiding your abilities, because smart, confident girls never pretend to be less than their best.

The End

There's not enough time to test another hypothesis, so you and Riley put together a presentation. Your results aren't earth-shattering, but you know that in science, that's normal. Scientists have to test and retest things all the time to learn the truth. Your experiment was a good first step, and you're proud of it.

You're even more proud when your friend Amber wins a first-place ribbon with an idea you passed along—an experiment to test whether dogs see color.

"I knew that idea was a winner!" you say, hugging Amber. "I'm so proud of you!"

"Well, it was your idea," Amber says. "I wish we could *both* get blue ribbons."

"That *was* a great idea for a project," Riley says. "Why didn't you use it yourself?"

You're not sure what to say. "You wanted to test your brainpower idea," you say hesitantly, "and I wanted to help."

"Even though you thought your own idea was a winner?" Riley asks.

She doesn't seem angry with you, just curious, so you decide to tell her the truth. "I didn't want to outshine you," you say, your eyes cast downward. "You were excited about your project, and I thought it might be awkward if I did something else—especially if I won without you."

Turn to page 86.

Suddenly you come to your senses. You're not going to let Devin ruin science for you—or come between you and your friends.

"Sure," you say to Logan. "I'd love to join you." Then you turn to the rest of the table. "How about you, Devin? Alexis? Does anyone else want to do the homework together?"

Devin lets out a snort. "No thanks," she says.

Alexis gives you an embarrassed smile. She kind of wants to join your study group, you can tell, but she'd probably never say so in front of Devin.

You're surprised, though, when Alexis knocks on your door a half hour later. She seems shy when she asks, "May I do homework with you and Logan?"

Turn to page 51.

You grab a piece of fruit and a muffin for Nadia before leaving the student center, and then you head to her room. She answers the door with a paintbrush in her hand. Her fingers are smeared with a rainbow of colors, and you're surprised to see that she's smiling.

"Are you okay?" you ask.

"I am now—I'm painting," Nadia says, waving her brush to invite you in. "This is how I de-stress. And after that math quiz, I definitely needed to get rid of some stress."

"Are you afraid you didn't do well?" you ask, already knowing the answer.

"I'm *sure* I didn't do well," Nadia says sadly. She takes a deep breath and adds, "The truth is, I'm not even supposed to be in that class. I was signed up for an easier class, but it conflicted with an abstract painting class I really wanted to take. So I switched to a math class that I wasn't ready for."

Suddenly everything is crystal clear. "No wonder you're having so much trouble!" you say.

"Not anymore," Nadia says with a rueful laugh. "I'm switching to the class I belong in."

Turn to page 53.

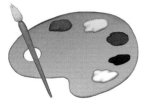

You and Alexis get together in your room to read the science chapter and answer the questions. Sure enough, Devin and Madison don't show up until after you've finished the work. When Devin reaches for your notebook to see what you've done, you feel frozen: you want to snatch back your notebook, but you can't move.

It's just this one time, you tell yourself as you watch Devin copy your answers.

Over the next week, though, it happens again—twice. Devin has plenty of compliments for you in class, calling you the "star scientist," but she also has plenty of excuses after class for why she can't do the homework.

When Ms. Blackwell announces this year's Innerstar U Science Fair, Devin just assumes that the two of you will team up. You don't want to be her partner, but if you tell her that, will she turn on you? You don't want to try to pull off a science-fair project in the middle of a fight with Devin.

 If you agree to be Devin's partner for the science fair, turn to page 73.

 If you let you her know you plan to work on your own project, turn to page 88.

You're beaming when you lead Alexis up the stairs to the attic in Brightstar House—the room where you and your friends usually study together.

Logan and Paige greet you both with a big hello. Soon you're taking turns reading aloud from the first chapter in your science book, which describes a simple experiment: testing whether yawns and smiles are contagious.

"Hey, let's try it!" Logan pipes up. You take turns yawning and smiling at each other, and pretty soon all four of you are yawning—and cracking up. Your conclusion? Yawns and smiles are *both* contagious!

Without Devin around, Alexis seems a lot more confident, and you discover that she's pretty fun to hang out with. Later, in your room, you start wondering why she hangs out with someone like Devin. You can't figure it out.

 Turn to page 70.

Logan nods her head. "Devin can be a bully," she says. "But if you give in to her now, it'll never stop. That'll be way more difficult than having a lab partner who's mad at you."

Paige agrees. "You need to find a way to show her that you're confident—that you think for yourself and make your own decisions," she says.

Right, you think. *But how exactly do I do that?*

 Turn to page 62.

A confident girl thinks for herself and makes her own decisions.

INNERSTAR UNIVERSITY

That's when you get a good look at the painting Nadia is working on. You can't make out what she painted exactly, but you love the way the colors swirl together.

"That's amazing!" you say. "What is it?"

"It's an abstract painting," Nadia explains. "Abstract art is more about expressing ideas and feelings than about making something look like it does in real life."

"Wow," you tell Nadia. "I never knew you were so talented."

Nadia's cheeks flush. "I don't know about talented," she says. "But I'm not as bad at *everything* as I am at math."

You bite your lip, wondering if you should talk about the quiz again. It seems better to stick with art. "I could never do anything like that," you say, nodding at the painting.

Nadia shakes her head. "I used to think that, too," she says. "But I learned to take a chance and just *paint*. Now I trust my hands and the paintbrush to say what I want them to say."

She reaches for a flyer on her desk and hands it to you. "I'm going to exhibit my new painting in this art show," she says. "You should enter something, too!"

Get Inspired!

 Turn to page 20.

Create a piece of art—a painting, a photograph, a sculpture, or something...

You can't wait for the weekend, when you can do your hamster experiment with Cheeks and Nibbles. For some reason, though, you don't tell Riley about it just yet.

For three days, you meet Riley after class to blow up soccer balls, let air out of soccer balls, kick soccer balls, and record soccer balls with your video camera. By the time the weekend hits, you're all soccered out. The only thing that perks you up is thinking about your hamster experiment.

On Friday afternoon, Ms. Blackwell helps you carry the hamsters' cage to your room. Before she leaves, she gives you strict instructions on how to care for Cheeks and Nibbles. Then she leaves, and it's time to get started!

 Turn to page 60.

When Alexis gets to your table and sits down, it's all you can do not to give her a huge hug. You know how hard it must have been for her to walk away from Devin. "Want to talk about it?" you ask.

Alexis shakes her head, and you and Logan give her the space she needs. After a few minutes, though, Alexis starts to perk up. When your friend Amber joins your table and shares a hilarious story about a new puppy at Pet-Palooza, Alexis laughs along with the rest of you.

By the time you all start walking back to Brightstar House, Alexis seems a whole lot happier. You hang back from the others for a minute to let her know how brave you think she was.

"Thanks," says Alexis. "I guess your confidence rubbed off on me."

You walk a few more steps in silence before Alexis says, "You know, I'll miss the fun side of being Devin's friend. But I'm not putting up with Devin the bully anymore. I'd rather hold out for a better friend."

Alexis gives you a shy, sideways glance, and you reach out to squeeze her hand. You both know that she's already found that friend—in you.

The End

"I'd better stick with what I'm good at," you tell Nadia. "Science and math are more my thing."

At the word *math*, Nadia's face falls. "You should know," she says reluctantly, "that I talked to Ms. Williams before coming back to my room. I told her everything—about how you've been helping me with our math homework. I'm sorry I put you in such a tough position."

You feel a flood of relief. You feel bad that Nadia didn't pass the quiz, but you're glad that her secret is finally out in the open—it was getting harder and harder to hide it.

Still, you're a little nervous. *Will I get in trouble with Ms. Williams for letting Nadia copy my work?* you wonder.

 Turn to page 64.

To keep the peace, you say to Devin, "I've got it. I can do the projects."

"Thanks—you're the best," Devin says.

But as she walks away, giggling with Madison, you kick yourself. *Why do girls do what she asks?* you wonder. *Why do I do what she asks?*

You're in deep now and can't find your way out, at least not on your own. You need a good friend to talk to.

It's Logan who comes to mind first. She gives good advice, and besides, you owe her and Paige an apology for not hanging out with them lately.

You find Logan in her room, and you're glad to see Paige there beside her, science book in hand.

As soon as you walk into the room, you open your mouth, and everything comes out in a rush. You tell Logan and Paige about doing Devin's work—and about how she wants you to do not just one science-fair project but two.

"I'm afraid if I say no to Devin, she'll make science class miserable for me," you say.

Turn to page 52.

The next afternoon in science, Nadia takes her seat at your lab table, grinning from ear to ear. "When I told my art teacher that I had to drop out of her abstract-painting class, she offered to meet with me privately," says Nadia. "She thinks I'm talented!"

"You *are* talented!" you say, giving her a hug.

Nadia ducks out of your hug and comes up grinning. "So, we have a date in the art studio after classes today, right?" she asks.

You take a deep breath and nod. Nadia was brave enough to admit she was struggling in math, and now it's time for you to be brave and try something new—art.

You're imagining what you might paint, wondering if you'll ever be able to create something as beautiful as Nadia's painting, when Ms. Blackwell calls your class to attention.

 Turn to page 65.

The first thing you do is put the hamsters through the maze without any clues to help them along. You call this the "control maze," just to see how long it takes them to get to the other end. Nibbles is a little faster than Cheeks, but not by much.

Then you add some visual clues to the maze: you use red tape to mark all the correct turns. When you test the hamsters again, the results are exciting. Both hamsters ran through the maze with the red tape about twenty percent faster than they did through the control maze!

Finally, you take off the red tape and rub some crushed mint leaves along the correct path in the maze. And when you run the hamsters through the maze this time, you can't believe the stopwatch in your hand. The hamsters ran through the scented maze thirty percent faster than they did through the control maze.

You repeat the experiment over the weekend, this time starting with the scented maze and then wiping off the mint scent and marking correct turns with red tape. Again, the hamsters are faster at making their way through the maze marked with mint than the maze marked with the red tape.

You decide that your hypothesis was right: hamsters follow their noses, or scented clues, better than visual cues. You proved something interesting, and you, Cheeks, and Nibbles had a lot of fun, too.

Turn to page 63.

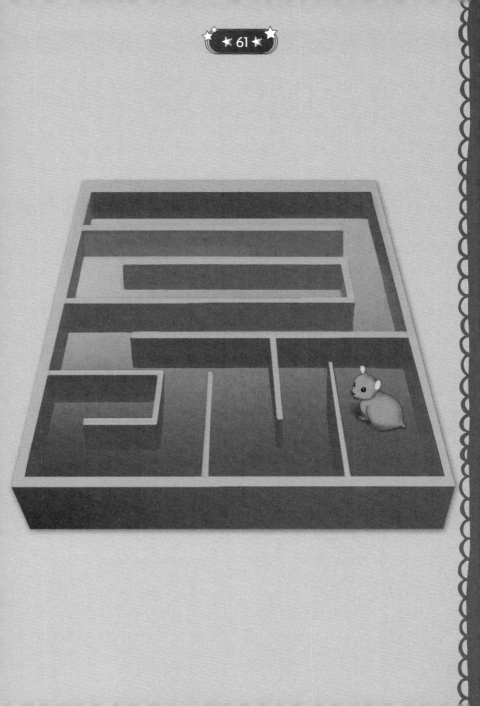

It's Logan who comes up with a solution, just as you hoped she would. "Why don't you try a little experiment?" she says. "Next time Devin wants you to do something for her, don't give in, and see what she does. Who knows? She might even be sweeter to you, because *she* needs this lab partnership to work out way more than you do."

You think about that for a moment and realize that it's kind of true. You've been doing Devin's work, which means she doesn't have a clue what's going on in science lab. How can she treat you badly now? She needs you!

Of course, you still have to test Logan's theory to be sure she's right. At lab the next day, you tell Devin that you're willing to work on a project with her for the science fair, but Alex and Madison are on their own.

Devin opens her mouth to snap at you, but you see the moment when she decides not to. "Whatever," she says, shrugging. "They can do their own."

What she's thinking, you're sure, is that at least you'll take care of *her* project. Devin doesn't realize, though, that after standing up to her once, you feel a whole lot more confident about standing up to her again. You're going to make sure she pulls her weight on this project, because if she doesn't, she's going to lose a pretty good science partner. You're much too valuable to push around.

The End

The question now is what to do with the results of your hamster experiment. The deadline for science-fair projects is coming quickly, but you can't enter one alongside Riley's, at least not without telling her.

As it turns out, you don't have to wonder what to do for long. While you're helping Riley put the finishing touches on her project, she confesses that she's not very happy with how it turned out.

"So flat balls don't bounce as high," she sighs. "I could have told you that before we got started."

You're trying to think of something comforting to say to Riley when Ms. Blackwell walks over and asks you when you're submitting *your* project.

"It's right here," Riley says, pointing to the soccer-ball poster.

"No, I mean the hamster project," Ms. Blackwell says directly to you.

Turn to page 66.

You decide to talk things over with Logan, who tutors other students sometimes. *Has she ever been in this situation?* you wonder.

When you get to Logan's room, you confess everything: how you gave Nadia the answers and pretended not to understand in class so that Nadia could have extra help.

Logan listens to your story, nodding her head knowingly. Then she says, "You just wanted to help a friend—I get that. But you should never be scared to do your best in class. Doing your best inspires other people to do the same."

 Turn to page 68.

Doing your best inspires others to do the same.

"I have a special announcement," Ms. Blackwell says. "It's time to sign up for next month's Innerstar U Science Fair."

Science fair? You feel a tingly rush of excitement. You have some great ideas for science-fair projects.

One of your classmates raises her hand. "Can we keep our same lab partners for the science fair?" she asks.

"You can enter with a partner or on your own," Ms. Blackwell tells her.

Out of the corner of your eye, you see Nadia turn to you. "Partners?" she whispers.

You pretend not to hear Nadia for a moment. Working with her in the lab has been fine, but do you want to be her partner for the science fair, too? She's so busy with her art that you could end up doing most of the work, and you'd have to share the credit. But if you say no, will things be awkward between you in lab?

After class, Nadia asks again if you'd like to be partners for the science fair.

 If you say yes to Nadia, turn to page 67.

 If you let Nadia know you'd rather work alone, turn to page 69.

Your face turns red, and you mumble something about turning in your project tomorrow. When Ms. Blackwell leaves, you have to tell Riley everything.

"A hamster project?" she says. "Why didn't you tell me? I love hamsters!"

Suddenly it occurs to you that you robbed Riley of a project that she might have enjoyed. And by hiding your good idea, you were robbing yourself of the fun of working with a friend, too.

After telling Riley the truth, you feel better. If she's not happy with her project, maybe it's not too late for her to be a part of yours.

"Do you want to see my hamster-project photos?" you ask her. "And help me make a poster, maybe?"

Riley agrees, and after class, you lead the way back to Brightstar House—determined to share the rest of your project and to *stop* hiding your good ideas.

The End

You don't think partnering with Nadia for the science fair is the best idea, but you don't want to hurt her feelings, and you still feel bad about what happened in math class.

"Sure, partner," you say. "I've got lots of ideas."

"Let's brainstorm in the art studio this afternoon," Nadia says. "I always do my best thinking with a paintbrush in my hand."

You can't imagine doing your best *anything* with a paintbrush in your hand, but you meet Nadia at Sparkle Studios after your last class. You don't think of yourself as creative. The only time you draw is when you have to illustrate something in your lab notebook.

Even so, you're amazed at all the creative things girls are doing at Sparkle Studios. In the computer lab, you spot Logan playing with digital art while another girl is editing photographs. You wave to your friends Shelby and Paige in the scrapbooking studio, and then you poke your head into the woodworking room, where you see a girl sanding a picture frame. You and Nadia linger for a while in the pottery room, too, where girls are creating ceramic vases.

 Turn to page 76.

You know Logan's right. You did pretend to be less than your best, and that didn't help Nadia at all. In fact, it hurt her. She would have gotten help from Ms. Williams a whole lot sooner if it hadn't been for you.

You decide to talk with Ms. Williams before class the next day. You just want to get it over with so that you can stop waiting for and worrying about her reaction.

As it turns out, Ms. Williams is understanding but stern. "Giving Nadia the answers was cheating," she says, "and it made Nadia feel even *less* confident about math. She can learn only if she does her own work."

You stare at the floor. "I know," you mumble. "I'm sorry."

Ms. Williams rests her hand on your shoulder. "I'm glad you learned something from this, too," she says. "Does that mean my best math student will be returning to class tomorrow?"

When you glance up, you see that Ms. Williams is smiling at you.

You nod and stand a little straighter. "Absolutely," you say. You hid your talents to try to help Nadia, but from here on out, you're going to polish them up and let them shine.

The End

Saying no to Nadia is awkward, but you'd really rather do a project on your own. You like the idea of being the lone scientist, working away in her lab, making amazing scientific breakthroughs.

"I'm sorry," you tell Nadia. "I have an idea for a project, and it's definitely a one-person job."

Nadia looks surprised, but she musters a smile. "No worries," she says.

When Nadia reminds you about your plan to do some painting at Sparkle Studios later, you shake your head.

"You know, with the science fair coming up, I don't think I'll have time for art, too," you tell her.

Nadia definitely looks disappointed now, and you feel a twinge of regret. But thinking about the science fair gives you the nudge you need to stick to your decision. This is your chance to shine!

 Turn to page 72.

You decide to come right out and ask Alexis why she's friends with a girl who's so mean to her. You walk back to Brightstar House and search for her room. It's not hard to find—there's a collage of horses on the door. You knock.

Alexis seems surprised to see you at her door, but she gives you a smile.

"What's up?" she asks.

"May I ask you an awkward question? It's about Devin," you say.

Alexis draws you inside and settles into one of her comfy chairs while you take the other one. She sighs, as if she can already guess your question.

"You want to know why I'm friends with Devin, right?" she asks. *Bull's-eye.*

"Yeah, I do," you tell her. "She's not very nice to you."

Turn to page 74.

Over the next three weeks, you spend every spare minute on your project. You're so convinced that your idea is a winner that you keep it a secret from everyone—even your friends. And you've already cleared a space on your bulletin board for your blue ribbon.

On the day of the science fair, you hurry across campus to the Market to set up your presentation early. You conducted an experiment to prove that sand from the beach at Starfire Lake contains meteor dust—a theory that your friend Logan told you about a few months ago. You're so excited. There's ancient stardust right here at Innerstar U!

Only *after* you make your presentation to the judges do you discover that Logan conducted almost the same experiment. If you hadn't been so afraid that someone would steal your idea, you would have talked about your project with your friends and figured out that you and Logan were doing the same thing. Then you could have chosen another project.

"I guess we should have compared notes ahead of time," Logan says with a laugh. "Oh, well. Let's go see what everyone else did."

Turn to page 75.

You reluctantly agree to be Devin's partner for the science fair, but you're not thrilled about it, especially when you discover over dinner that she wants you to work on two projects—one for you and Devin and one for Alexis and Madison.

"Madison and I have a riding competition to get ready for," Devin says. "You've got this, right? Alexis will help you."

Got this? you think. No. What you've *got* is a serious problem, you realize now. You look across the dining hall to see Logan and Paige sitting with Riley—girls who would never bully you or ask you to do their work for them. Can you find your way back to them? Or do you have to keep playing this game with Devin, at least until the end of the science lab?

 If you say no to Devin, turn to page 78.

 If you agree to do two science-fair projects, turn to page 58.

Alexis shrugs. "Sometimes she's really nice," she says. "And other times she's not. Right now, she's being kind of a pain, but it'll pass, and we'll be best friends again."

Something about Alexis's hopeful expression makes your heart hurt. "But is that any way for her to treat her best friend?" you have to ask.

"You don't understand," Alexis says in a frustrated voice. "Devin was my *first* friend here, and she got me involved with the riding team. I can't just stop being her friend."

"I'm sorry," you say quickly. "I didn't mean to make you feel worse. I just wondered."

Alexis is quiet for a moment, and then she tries again. You can tell that she really wants you to understand.

"I wasn't very popular at my old school," she says. "I was so quiet and shy that I hardly had any friends. Devin changed that. If I'm not friends with Devin anymore, I'll lose my other friends, too—like Madison."

 Turn to page 82.

There are lots of exciting projects to look at, but you're surprised to see that Nadia's impresses you the most! She used combinations of colored lights to show how the eye sees color.

Not only is her idea interesting, but it's totally creative, just like Nadia. You're not surprised when the judges announce that she's the winner. She deserves it.

"Congratulations, science star!" you say to Nadia, giving her a big hug.

You're happy for Nadia, but at the same time, you're a little upset with yourself. You were so confident that you were a better scientist than Nadia that you never even listened to her ideas. You missed out on a chance to work on a fun and creative project with a good friend. Next time, you'll be more open to other people's ideas.

The End

After pointing out all the different things you could try, Nadia leads you to her favorite studio of all—the painting studio. There are giant windows along the walls, letting in lots of light and offering great views of campus.

Some girls, including your friend Neely, are already painting. Neely's so absorbed in her work that she barely looks up to say hi.

Nadia points toward two easels with blank canvases. "Let's get started!" she says.

Get started? you wonder. *I can't even remember how.*
It feels like forever since you last took an art class. And
watching all the other girls paint kind of intimidates you.
Maybe you should just stick with what you know best and
get to work on that science-fair project.

 If you ask Nadia for help with painting, turn to page 79.

 If you let her know that art just isn't your thing,
turn to page 80.

"No, Devin," you say quietly but firmly. "I *don't* have this."

You catch the look of surprise—and the hint of a smile—on Alexis's face.

Devin arches an eyebrow. "What's the problem?" she asks, her voice edgy.

"I'm not doing your work anymore," you say. And with those words, you suddenly feel a lot braver.

"Then maybe you need to find a new group of friends to sit with," Devin snaps.

You stand and scoop up your dinner tray. "No problem. I have plenty of friends," you say. But as you walk across the cafeteria, you start to wonder about that. *Do* you still have friends? Or did you lose them all when you started hanging out with Devin?

You walk slowly toward Logan and Paige, wondering how you can make things up to them. Logan glances up and catches you looking at her, and for a long, painful moment, she just stares back. Then she does something small that's also incredibly kind. She slides over on the bench to make room for you.

There's not a lot of space there, but it's enough—and when you slide in, you get to work apologizing to your friends. By the time dinner's over, you feel a whole lot better, but there's one person you're still worried about—Alexis. Is she happy being Devin's friend?

 Turn to page 70.

When Nadia sees the look on your face, you don't even have to ask for help. "Don't you ever paint?" she asks.

"I finger-painted in kindergarten," you admit. "And I've done a few paintings in art class—when I had to. But I haven't painted in a really long time. I can't remember how to start."

"I'm an abstract painter," Nadia says. "I just pick up a brush, think about what I want to say, and let my creativity take over. You could start with a sketch, if that's easier for you."

You're not sure that *would* be easier, but you're willing to give it a try. You pick up a pencil from the tray of the easel, but that's as far as you get. "What should I sketch?" you ask.

Nadia grins. "I don't know! Something that *inspires* you," she says. "Try not to think about it—just put your pencil to the canvas and go."

You take a deep breath and lower your pencil. "Actually, I think I'll just watch for a while," you say.

Nadia shrugs. "Suit yourself," she says as she dips her brush into paint.

 Turn to page 81.

"Thanks for trying to help me," you tell Nadia. "But art just isn't my thing. I'd rather stick with the science-fair project."

Nadia pauses and then says, "Are you sure? There are lots of different things you could do for the show. You don't have to paint."

"I'm sure," you tell her, wrinkling your nose. "I'd be terrible. But you're an amazing artist. I can't wait to see what you create!"

On the day of the art show, you're impressed by everyone's work—especially Nadia's painting of the fountain at Five-Points Plaza, which is alive with color and light. But nothing is more surprising than an entry in the teacher's section—a giant question-mark drawing submitted by your science teacher, Ms. Blackwell!

When you take a closer look, you see that the question mark is made up of sketches of famous women scientists and their breakthroughs.

"Wow," you tell her. "I didn't know you were so creative. I think of you as a scientist, not an artist."

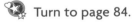 Turn to page 84.

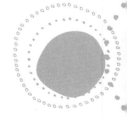

You stand back and watch Nadia paint. You can tell that painting makes her feel happy and strong. She's as confident in the art studio as you are in the science lab. It's fun to watch her doing something that comes so easily for her.

Every once in a while Nadia looks out the window, and you soon realize that she's painting an abstract picture of the star-shaped fountain at Five-Points Plaza. Her hand is so sure that sometimes she doesn't even glance back at the canvas. It's as if she can see the painting without looking at it, and that gives you an idea for a science-fair project.

You've often heard that when people lose one of their five senses, such as sight or hearing, their other senses get even stronger. You're wondering how you could test someone's hearing or sense of smell when you remember the sandpaper in the woodworking studio—and another idea hits you.

 Turn to page 85.

You can see that Alexis feels torn, and you tell her that you understand—even though you're not really sure you do. You leave her room feeling sad for her, wishing you could help her find the confidence to stand up to Devin. Maybe there *are* some things you can do.

Over the next few weeks, you're firm with Devin about doing her own homework and her share of the work in lab. But even better, you make a point of being a friend to Alexis and invite her to join you when you're hanging out with your other friends.

One night at dinner, you overhear Devin making fun of Alexis from your seat at the next table. You meet Alexis's eyes and can see that she's fighting back tears. And then something magical happens: Alexis gets up from her seat next to Devin and leaves the table. You and Logan wave her over to your table, and Alexis walks toward you, slowly but steadily.

 Turn to page 56.

"Who says scientists aren't creative?" Ms. Blackwell asks. "All of the great scientific breakthroughs started with a creative leap—a question. What if the earth is round instead of flat? Can we create a lens to help us see things that are too small to see with our own eyes? Can humans fly—into space?"

Wow, you never thought of it like that. "I thought science was all about trying to find the right answers," you admit to Ms. Blackwell. "And I thought if I tried to do something creative, like art, I'd get it way *wrong*."

Ms. Blackwell laughs. Then she says gently, "A real scientist—like a real artist—doesn't let a thing like fear of failure stop her from trying something new."

You nod—you get it now. Out of the corner of your eye, you catch sight of a "Get Inspired!" sign over the exhibit doorway. For the first time, you actually *do* feel a little bit inspired about this art thing.

You find Nadia in front of her gorgeous painting. She's a good friend, and you have a feeling she'll be a great teacher, too.

"I'm ready to try," you say. "How about a painting lesson after science tomorrow?"

The End

"Hey, Nadia!" you say. "What if we do an experiment about how our sense of sight affects our sense of touch?"

Nadia breaks her gaze away from the fountain and turns toward you. It takes her a minute to process what you said. She must have *really* been into her work!

"That sounds interesting," Nadia finally says. "How would it work, though?"

"Sandpaper comes in different grades, from really fine to really coarse, right?" you ask.

"I don't know. I guess so," Nadia says slowly.

"We'll have people touch and rate different kinds of sandpaper," you explain. "Then we'll blindfold them for a while—maybe an hour or two—and have them rate the papers again to see if their sense of touch is better when they don't have their sight."

Nadia nods, her brow furrowed in concentration. "But do you think it'll really change?" she asks.

"I don't know," you answer honestly. "That's what we want to find out!"

Nadia smiles. "Okay!" she says. "I'm in. And maybe we can get our friends to help out."

 Turn to page 87.

Riley's jaw drops. "I would *never* be mad at you for winning," she says, "especially if you had a better project than I did. A friend who wants you to do less than your best isn't really a friend, right?"

Right, you realize now. If you'd had more confidence in yourself and your friendship with Riley, then you would have known that from the beginning. Next time, you promise yourself, you'll do your best—and trust Riley and your other friends to support you all the way.

The End

A friend who wants you to do less than your best isn't really a friend.

Nadia's excited about your science-project idea, but she's not ready to leave the studio yet. "Now that we figured out our project, don't you want to pick up a paintbrush and see how your senses of sight and touch work together?" she jokes.

You laugh. "I guess I could pretend it's an experiment," you say. You pick up a brush, but it feels awkward in your hand. You still don't know how to start. Math and science seem to be more about finding the right answers. With art, there are no right or wrong answers—just creativity.

Nadia can see that you're still stuck. "Wait, I have an idea!" she says. She unties the scarf she's wearing and ties it over your eyes. Then she puts a brush in your hand. "Now, *paint!*"

Giggling, you reach forward and put a few brushstrokes on the canvas. Every few minutes, Nadia washes your brush, dips it in a different color of paint, and hands it back to you. When she finally takes off your blindfold, you see that you created a big, colorful mess. But the experiment definitely helped you loosen up and have some fun with art.

 If you're inspired to pick up a pencil and try sketching, turn to page 89.

 If you think it's time to start that science-fair project, turn to page 92.

"Thanks for the offer," you tell Devin. "But I want to enter the science fair on my own this year. I have a great idea, but it's definitely a one-person project."

You see the look of surprise cross Devin's face, and you brace yourself for a nasty comment. Devin's not happy, but she can't turn on you if she expects you to keep handing over your science homework.

After class you walk over to Pet-Palooza, a pet shop and day-care center on campus, to get permission to conduct your experiment. You want to learn whether dogs see color or whether they're completely color-blind. You always suspected that Rascal, your dog at home, recognized the yellow container that held his doggie treats.

Your friend Amber, the head volunteer at Pet-Palooza, introduces you to the manager. They both think your project is a great idea. You gather your materials, open a notebook, and write "Hypothesis: Dogs See Some Color."

Turn to page 90.

What you painted isn't exactly a masterpiece, but it was kind of a fun experiment, you think. And when you look at it that way, you're eager to try more.

You pick up a pencil and look out the same window as Nadia. You have a great view of Five-Points Plaza. Some girls are walking through it. Others are hanging out on the benches, chatting. The water is sparkling in the sunshine. It's almost as if *it's* laughing, right along with the girls.

You spot a head of curly red hair bobbing along the path by the fountain. Isabel! And the black-haired girl walking next to her looks like Emmy. Both Isabel and Emmy are good friends, and you've spent lots of time with them, hanging out in Five-Points Plaza.

The fountain inspires you just as much as it does Nadia, because it reminds you of the great friends you've met here at Innerstar U, all with different strengths and talents that inspire you, too. But can you express all that in a picture?

Nadia sees your hesitation. "You have an idea, right?" she says, her eyes dancing. "Go for it! You can do it," she says.

 Turn to page 94.

You start with a golden retriever puppy named Honey. While Amber watches, you lead the puppy to a quiet part of the play area and let her explore two containers full of doggie treats. One has a yellow sticker on the front, and the other has a red sticker on the front. Otherwise, the containers are exactly the same.

After two minutes, you open the yellow container and give Honey a treat.

You repeat this every day for a week, changing the position of the containers but always giving Honey a treat from the yellow container. Soon, Honey heads directly for the yellow container. She sees yellow!

You make a few notes and then hurry home to drop your notebook off in your room and head to dinner. When you return to your room *after* dinner, you're surprised to find Devin sitting at your desk.

"Your door was unlocked, and I didn't think you'd mind," she says, waving your science book. "I left mine at the stables by mistake, so I'm reading yours."

You're even more surprised now, hearing that Devin is reading a chapter instead of just asking you what it was about. Maybe your interest in science is starting to rub off on your partner.

Turn to page 100.

You step back to admire your masterpiece. "Well, it's original, anyway," you say to Nadia with a laugh. "But from here on out, I'm going to let *you* handle the art. I think I'm better off focusing on our science-fair project."

Nadia grins, and the two of you make a plan to start the science-fair project tomorrow.

The next day, you get to lab early, before Nadia, and see that Ms. Blackwell has already written your assignment on the whiteboard. You begin the experiment, jotting notes in your notebook as you go.

This is your favorite part of science—measuring the ingredients in test tubes and beakers and combining them to create something new. You see your reflection in the window. In your white lab coat and safety goggles, beaker in hand, you look like a real scientist! And it's kind of fun to work on your own again without waiting for Nadia to carefully record all the steps in her notebook.

 Turn to page 35.

This painting is supposed to express what inspires you, and science is definitely on that list. So you choose a tiny brush and exactly the right shade of blue, but instead of simply painting in the water, you fill the pool with tiny H_2Os—the scientific symbol for water.

When Nadia sees what you're doing, she's impressed.

"Cool!" she says. "You could use different shades of blue to help create light and shadows, and even add some white for the sprays of the fountain," she suggests.

"Great idea, thanks!" you tell her.

It's a long, slow process, filling in all those tiny symbols, but it's worth it. When you step back from your painting, all you see is a pool of water. The H_2Os are clear only when you look very closely.

 Turn to page 102.

You don't share Nadia's confidence in your artistic talents, but you do ask yourself a question: *if a scientist was going to create a picture that expressed what inspires her, what would it look like?*

Suddenly, you get an idea! You head over to the scrap-booking studio and find a ruler. Next, with scientific precision, you use it to draw the sharp edges of the star-shaped fountain's paths on a blank canvas. Then you empty out a can that was holding paintbrushes, and you trace the can to draw the round pool beneath the star, along with the benches that circle it.

You're about to start filling in your sketch with paint when another idea hits you. What if you brought a little science into the painting by incorporating some scientific names and symbols?

If you decide to bring science into your painting, turn to page 93.

If you simply paint your sketch, turn to page 98.

You're kind of impatient with Nadia for interrupting, but you stop what you're doing to hear what she has to say.

"You missed three steps," she says, pointing back and forth between your notebook and the whiteboard.

Your cheeks flush when you check the board. Nadia is right. You were racing to finish first instead of being careful. You didn't even wait for your partner to get to class before you got started!

"I'm sorry," you tell her. "I should have waited for you. You just saved our experiment from going way wrong. Thanks, partner."

Instead of being angry with you, Nadia seems happy. "Wow," she says. "That's the first time I really *felt* like your partner—like I could do more than just take notes. I'm actually starting to like science. You must be rubbing off on me!"

Now it's your turn to feel good. When Nadia asked you to be her lab partner, she didn't have confidence in her ability to do well in science, and now she does. "I'm glad that we're going to be partners for the science fair," you tell her, and this time you really mean it.

Turn to page 99.

You're sure you know what you're doing. You go ahead and add the water to the beaker. "Write down 'eight ounces of H_2O,'" you tell Nadia.

Instantly, the mixture in the beaker begins to fizz and form a thick, foul-smelling potion. It bubbles up over the top of the beaker and starts to spill over onto the floor. That wasn't supposed to happen! You watch, horrified, while the girls around you plug their noses and run for the door.

"Everybody out!" Ms. Blackwell orders, grabbing the lab notebook from Nadia's hand.

"I'm—I'm sorry," you sputter. "I don't know what went wrong."

Ms. Blackwell quickly reads over your notes. "You didn't create anything toxic," she says, looking relieved, "but you skipped three steps in the experiment and made a big mess. How is it that neither one of you realized that?"

You check the board and see that Nadia was right. You were so sure you knew what you were doing that you didn't double-check. Worse yet, you ignored Nadia's warnings.

Turn to page 104.

You decide to simply fill in your sketch with paint. It's the first painting you've done in a long time, after all, so you don't want to get too fancy. Plus, you're not sure how a painting made up of scientific names and symbols would go over at an art show.

On the day of the show, you're nervous but excited to show off your painting. Walking through the exhibit, you see that lots of girls incorporated unusual things in their artwork. Paige used real leaves in her nature collage, for instance. It's beautiful, and it really reminds you of the artist who made it. You're kind of sorry now that you didn't bring more science into your painting.

Entering my painting in the art show was a big leap, you remind yourself. You're proud of yourself for trying something new. But next time, you'll have more confidence in your ideas—and really get inspired!

The End

After science lab, you tell Nadia that you'll go get sand-paper for your science-fair project and will meet her back in your room in an hour. You stop by the woodworking room in Sparkle Studios and pick out six different grades of sandpaper. You can see that some are much finer than others, but when you close your eyes and try to tell which is which with your fingertips, you discover that it's really tough to do.

When you get back to your room, you tape the sand-paper to your desk and open a new notebook to the first page. You carefully write: "Hypothesis: Loss of sight results in a more sensitive sense of touch."

While you're waiting for Nadia, you jot down the steps of your experiment and a list of girls you plan to ask to be test subjects.

Turn to page 103.

Over the next two weeks, Devin seems more interested in class and actually does her own homework. You're relieved, because you're super busy with your science project.

You repeat your experiment with Honey using other colors. She takes longer to recognize blue than yellow, and even longer to see red. Then you test two other puppies, a Westie named Coconut and an English bulldog named Meatloaf. You get the same results. Your conclusion? Dogs see shades of yellow and blue but are less sensitive to seeing red.

The morning of the science fair, you wake up with butterflies in your stomach, but you're excited about your project. You want to do a great job in honor of your four-legged friends.

 Turn to page 110.

You keep working on the sandpaper experiment. *It was my idea in the first place,* you tell yourself, *and it's still a good one.*

You conduct your experiment using three friends as test subjects, but you don't feel very confident about your results. Neely does better using her sight and touch together than she does after being blindfolded for ninety minutes. The same is true for Logan. Only Isabel does a better job of rating the sandpapers after being blindfolded. That's not at all what you expected.

At the science fair, the judges look over your results. "Were girls able to see the differences in the sandpapers in the first test?" asks one of the judges. You slowly nod. It's almost exactly the same question Nadia asked you, which feels like a blow to the stomach. Nadia was right to worry about that, and you should have listened to her.

When you agreed to be Nadia's partner, you thought that she needed you more than you needed her. But that wasn't true—you needed each other.

Every good scientist needs someone to ask questions and make sure she's following the right procedures. You forgot that. If Nadia gives you another chance, you'll do your best to be a better science partner—and a better friend.

The End

Over the next couple of weeks, you come back to the studio a few times to finish the painting. Nadia helps you paint a dark-haired girl and a redhead walking by the bubbling fountain. You fill the sky with "O_2," the symbol for oxygen, painted in blues and grays. And you make a pattern on the girls' clothes by repeating the word *Homo sapiens*.

When you're done, you're so excited about the painting that you decide to enter it in the art show. You can't wait to show it off! Your painting hangs right next to Nadia's. Hers is wild and abstract, full of creative joy. Yours is more realistic, but it's creative, too. It shows everyone what inspires you—science, Innerstar U, friends, and even art.

Ms. Blackwell is the first person to look really closely at your painting and spot the scientific names and symbols. "Great job," she tells you. "What a creative way to combine science and art!"

You smile at Nadia, and she beams back at you. She gave you the confidence to try something new. Thanks to her, you're an artist.

But Ms. Blackwell's next comment reminds you that you're supposed to be a scientist, too: "I can't wait to see what you two are doing for the science fair."

Uh-oh. You've been so busy with your painting that you haven't made any progress on your experiment!

Turn to page 105.

When Nadia knocks on your door, you invite her in and show her the six different grades of sandpaper taped to your desk. You explain how the experiment is supposed to work: Girls will touch the sandpapers and rate them from finest to coarsest. Then you'll put a blindfold over their eyes for a while and test them again.

"How long will they wear the blindfold?" Nadia asks.

"Maybe an hour," you say. Then you think about it a bit more. "Ninety minutes might be better."

Your hypothesis is that girls will be better at feeling the differences in the sandpapers after being without sight.

"Won't girls be able to see the differences in the sand-papers in the first test?" she asks.

Nadia's question catches you off guard. It doesn't sound as if she trusts that you know what you're doing. Did she lose confidence in you after what happened in the lab today? You wonder how you can convince her that your experiment is a solid one.

 If you stop to consider Nadia's question, turn to page 106.

 If you confidently dismiss the question, turn to page 107.

While you help Ms. Blackwell open some windows, you explain to her what happened.

Ms. Blackwell gives you a stern look. "Confidence is a good quality to have," she says, "but overconfidence, especially in a laboratory, can be dangerous. You should have listened to Nadia. Partners in a science lab need to know they can trust each other."

You accept your punishment—cleaning up the mess you made—with a big dose of humility.

"I'm sorry I didn't listen to you," you say to Nadia, who is trying to salvage what's left of her wet notebook.

"It's my fault, too," she says. "I always let you do all the work. I leaned on you too much, so you probably thought I wasn't that interested."

"Well, I didn't give you much of chance," you say. "From now on, I'll listen more."

Nadia smiles. "And I'll be more involved— starting right now," she says, grabbing a sponge from the bucket Ms. Blackwell brings you.

You reach for the mop, knowing that cleaning the mess is the easy part. You've got an uphill battle to prove to your teacher that you can be trusted in the lab. But you'll have a partner, Nadia, to help make sure you get things right.

The End

Right after the art show, you meet with Nadia to talk about the science fair. "Should we get started on the blindfold experiment?" she asks.

"There's no time!" you say. "I don't think we can ask our friends to help us when they're busy trying to finish their own projects. I got so caught up in my painting that I never stopped to think about how much time the experiment would take." You start to panic.

"Could we test each other?" Nadia suggests.

You shake your head. "Testing only two people won't give us valid results," you say.

"Okay then," Nadia says, shrugging. "Let's choose a different experiment."

You chew on your lip, thinking for a moment. "I've always thought that birds are more active in the morning than at any other time of day," you say. "What if we recorded their singing throughout the day to see if that's true?"

Nadia nods. "There's a fish experiment I remember reading about in our science book, too," she says. "We could study whether goldfish are more active living with plants in their bowls or with just plain water."

 If you decide to study fish, turn to page 108.

 If you decide to study birds, turn to page 112.

When you glance down at the sandpaper, you see that Nadia is right. You can tell a fine grade from a coarse one just by looking.

"What should we do?" you ask. "There must be a way to test this."

Nadia thinks about it for a minute. "What if we cover the sandpaper with a box and leave an opening for hands?" she asks.

"That's a great idea!" you say, and Nadia beams.

Over the next few nights, you test your friends. Some of them take the sandpaper test first while blindfolded and then again without the blindfold. Others take the test first without the blindfold and then again with it. In both groups, your subjects are better at rating sandpaper after being blindfolded. The experiment worked! Nadia's good questions and your willingness to listen made for a great project.

The morning of the science fair, the two of you set up your presentation together, confident that you're ready for any questions the judges might throw your way.

The End

"They *should* be able to see the sandpaper for the first test," you tell Nadia.

"But then we aren't really testing their sense of touch in the first experiment," she argues. "We're testing their sense of sight and touch combined."

Nadia's kind of acting like a know-it-all, which irritates you. *You're* the one who's better at science, after all. So you brush off her comment with a short response. "It's fine, Nadia," you say. "Just trust me, okay?"

Nadia seems hurt by your response. She clams up and doesn't say anything else, and after that night, your partnership starts to crumble. Nadia misses science lab the next day, and by the end of the week, she asks if it's okay if she does her own project. She thinks it might be better if you each enter the science fair on your own, without a partner.

Now you're the one who's hurt, but maybe you're a little relieved, too. Isn't this what you wanted?

 Turn to page 101.

You like Nadia's idea and think it might be easier than recording birdsong. You head right away to Pet-Palooza in the Shopping Square to buy goldfish, fish food, two fishbowls, and plants to fill one bowl.

Your plan is to prove that fish are more energetic when they're surrounded by plants.

The girl working at Pet-Palooza recommends that you let the water sit in the bowl overnight before adding the fish so that any harmful minerals evaporate or settle to the bottom. When you get back to Nadia's room, you fill both fishbowls with water and add plants to just one of the bowls. You let the water stand overnight and plan to start your experiment in the morning.

The next day, you stop by Nadia's room on your way to breakfast, and you help her slip the fish out of their plastic bags and into the fishbowls.

Turn to page 115.

You're shocked when you arrive at the science fair and see Devin setting up her presentation. The title of her poster reads "Hypothesis: Dogs See Some Color."

Devin stole your idea! And she must have copied the results of your experiment when she was alone in your room. The worst part is, she doesn't seem to feel the least bit guilty about it. She gives you a smug smile.

Your hands shake as you wipe away angry tears. You'd love to get Devin into trouble—big trouble—but you can't accuse her of stealing without proof. You take deep breaths and try to calm down while you set up your own presentation. You're careful to keep your Coconut and Meatloaf posters facedown so that Devin can't see them—not until after the judges do.

They stop at Devin's table first, and you walk over to hear her presentation. She claims to have conducted the experiment with her family's dog last summer. What a joke!

When one of the judges asks Devin if she repeated the experiment with other dogs, she says no. When a second judge questions Devin's scientific procedure, she can only stammer nervously.

At least she didn't copy my entire experiment, you think.

 Turn to page 113.

You think that testing your hypothesis about birdsong is something you and Nadia can do quickly and easily. You push for that idea, and Nadia agrees.

On Saturday, you bring a tape recorder to a peaceful spot on campus—a far corner of Morningstar Meadow, near a clump of trees. You visit the spot at dawn, at noon, and at dusk, recording the birdsong you hear.

After recording the birds for a day, you learn that the birds were definitely noisiest at dawn. *Are they chirping good morning?* you wonder. *Or letting each other know where the juiciest worms can be found?*

The birds were almost as noisy at dusk and were quietest at noon.

 If you continue recording the birds for another day, turn to page 114.

 If you rely on one day's research, turn to page 116.

You walk back over to your table without another glance at Devin. You're still angry, but you're relieved that you did a lot more work after Devin copied your test results.

A few minutes later, the judges arrive at your table, and you unveil your Coconut and Meatloaf posters next to your poster about Honey.

One of the judges smiles. "I see you didn't stop at just one dog," she says. And when she asks about your scientific procedure, you're able to outline all your steps and point to a graph on one of your posters.

As the judges move on, Ms. Blackwell steps up to the table and compliments you on your clear, confident presentation.

Later, when the judges present you with a blue ribbon, you look across the aisle at Devin. You're tempted to give her the same smug smile she gave you earlier, but you don't want to ruin this moment. Your hard work made you a winner, and there's nothing Devin—or anyone—can do to "steal" the way you feel right now.

The End

You and Nadia record birdsong again on Sunday with similar results. That gives you just one night to create your presentation, but you can do it. You stay up late, printing out photos of birds from the Internet, typing the steps of your experiment into a presentation, and creating a poster.

As you and Nadia decorate the poster together, you're tempted to make it a real work of art. You think about all those amazing projects you saw girls creating in the art studios. You glance at Nadia, who is one of the most creative girls you know, and then you glance at the clock. Do you have time to make this a great science poster *and* a great piece of art?

 If you want to make your science project a work of art, turn to page 118.

 If you decide that you've done enough for one night, turn to page 119.

You and Nadia settle in to watch the fish for a while. During the first hour, both goldfish behave the same way. They swim around the bowls, exploring their new homes.

But later in the day, when you check on your fish between classes, the fish in the bowl with the plants seems to be moving around more than the other fish.

By the next morning, the fish in the bowl with the plants is *definitely* more energetic than the other fish.

"Wow, this one seems really bored," says Nadia, her face pressed up against the glass of the bowl without plants.

You prop your chin on your hand and watch the fish for a while, too. "Definitely bored," you say. "I'm falling asleep just watching him!"

You make a few final notes and take some photos of both fish.

 Turn to page 117.

You rely on one day's research—it's all you have time for, isn't it?

On the day of the fair, you and Nadia hurry to the Market to set up your presentation. You can't help noticing how much more impressive most of the other projects are. It's obvious—at least to you—that you chose an easy idea and then rushed through the experiment.

Your stomach is full of butterflies while you and Nadia give your presentation. When the judges ask you some questions about your research, you have to admit you didn't retest your conclusions.

When they finally walk away, you slump against the table. "I'm glad that's over," you say. "I was so nervous!"

"Really?" Nadia asks. "You didn't seem nervous at all. You were so clear and calm. I was wishing I could be as confident as you."

You let Nadia's words sink in. It's true that even though you weren't thrilled with your experiment, you stuck with it and tried to present it well. It sort of reminds you of how you entered a painting in the art exhibit a week or so ago, even though you never thought you could do something like that.

Now you really *do* feel more confident. Is that what happens when you face your fears and try something new? *If so,* you think, *bring it on!*

The End

On the day of the science fair, you and Nadia present your board showing photos of the active fish surrounded by plants and the bored fish in the plain water. When Ms. Blackwell stops by your presentation, she nods but doesn't seem very excited. "So, you ended up with the same findings as those in your textbook, right?" she asks.

You nod, feeling a little embarrassed.

"I expected something a little more ambitious from you two," she says. "Especially after those great art projects. I'd love to see you bring that same creativity to your science experiments."

When Ms. Blackwell moves on to the next table, you and Nadia are quiet for a moment. "Sorry," you mumble to your friend.

But Nadia's not sorry. She says exactly what you need to hear: "Our science project might not be the best one in the room, but did you hear what Ms. Blackwell said about our art projects? You didn't even think you liked art. You should be proud of yourself for having the confidence to try something new."

Nadia's pep talk gives you a boost. "You're right," you say to her with a smile. "Next year, we're going for the blue ribbon—in *both* art and science!"

The End

When you ask Nadia if she wants to do something creative with the poster, she jumps all over the idea. Instead of one poster, you work on three—birds at dawn, at midday, and at dusk. You love the way Nadia paints the sun going down and the moon rising over Starfire Lake.

By the time you finish and Nadia heads for her room, you're both exhausted.

The next morning, the day of the science fair, you're so tired that you sleep right through your alarm. You're dreaming about  chirping birds when you stretch and slowly open your eyes. It's eleven o'clock—the fair started two hours ago! You run to Nadia's room, only to discover that she overslept, too.

You rush over to the Market with your project, but it's too late. You've missed the presentations. You flop down in the grass with a sigh. "I guess we should have done a basic, boring poster and gone to bed early," you mumble.

Nadia agrees. "Early bird gets the worm," she says.

There's a moment of silence, and then you both crack up. The truth is, you and Nadia had a blast getting creative with your science project. Maybe you're starting to like art almost as much as you like science. This could be the beginning of a beautiful friendship—after a good night's sleep!

The End

As much as you'd like to turn your bird project into a work of art, you have to be realistic. If you want to do well at the science fair tomorrow, you need sleep. *And our project is a good one,* you tell yourself, *with or without a fancy poster.*

You and Nadia finish your poster and get to bed early. The next morning, you hurry to the Market—the site of the science fair.

As you and Nadia set up your presentation, you can't help noticing that it's a little basic compared to some of the others. You spent so much time in the art studios before beginning your experiment that you didn't leave enough time to be creative afterward.

You and Nadia earn a third-place ribbon for your project anyway—which feels pretty good. And afterward, when Nadia asks if you want to paint with her at Sparkle Studios, you say yes. From here on out, you decide, you're going to try to make enough time for science *and* art.

The End